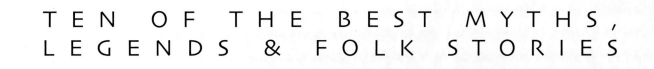

TEN OF THE BEST MYTHS,
LEGENDS & FOLK STORIES

TEN OF THE BEST
PRINCE AND
PRINCESS STORIES

DAVID WEST

Crabtree Publishing Company
www.crabtreebooks.com

Crabtree Publishing Company
www.crabtreebooks.com
1-800-387-7650

Publishing in Canada
616 Welland Ave.
St. Catharines, ON
L2M 5V6

Published in the United States
PMB 59051, 350 Fifth Ave.
59th Floor,
New York, NY

Published in **2015 by CRABTREE PUBLISHING COMPANY.**

Printed in the U.S.A./092014/JA20140811

Created and produced by:
   David West Children's Books

Project development, design, and concept:
   David West Children's Books

Author and designer: David West

Illustrator: David West

Editor: Anastasia Suen

Proofreader: Wendy Scavuzzo

Production coordinator and Prepress technicians:
   Samara Parent, Margaret Amy Salter

Print coordinator: Katherine Berti

Library and Archives Canada Cataloguing in Publication

West, David, 1956-, author
   Ten of the best prince and princess stories / David West.

(Ten of the best : myths, legends & folk stories)
Includes index.
Issued in print and electronic formats.
ISBN 978-0-7787-0787-5 (bound).--ISBN 978-0-7787-1460-6 (pbk.).--
ISBN 978-1-4271-7746-9 (pdf).--ISBN 978-1-4271-7738-4 (html)

   1. Fairy tales. I. Title. II. Title: Prince and princess stories.

PZ8.W473Te 2014   j398.2   C2014-903862-3
                                           C2014-903863-1

Library of Congress Cataloging-in-Publication Data

CIP available at Library of Congress

THE STORIES

 The Lake Princess

This is a story of how a general's servant became friends with a mysterious princess.

A long time ago, a general was fishing on Tung Lake. He saw a huge fish, and shot it with an arrow. The fish was pulled from the water, but the general's servant Chen could not bear to watch the fish die.

"Please may I put the fish back?" he pleaded.

After Chen persisted, the general relented and allowed him to return it to the lake. Chen even put a bandage on the fish's wound.

A year later, Chen was traveling on his own across the lake when his boat sank in a storm. He managed to make it to the shore where he passed out from exhaustion under a tree.

When he awoke, the storm had passed. Hiding beneath the tree, he saw a beautiful princess ride by. She was out hunting and was followed by her attendants. After they left, Chen wandered off until he came to a magnificent palace. He entered the courtyard and was immediately captured by guards.

As he was dragged before the princess, Chen thought he was going to be put to death for trespassing. When the princess saw him, her face lit up in amazement.

"Please forgive my rude guards," she said. "And accept my love and gratitude."

Chen could not believe his ears. "Thank you Princess, but I don't know what I have done to deserve this," he replied.

"Last year, I was wounded by an arrow. But you saved me," she explained. "And you even put a bandage on my wound."

"Ah, so you were the fish I saved!" said Chen. From that day on, the princess and the servant were the best of friends.

People who change from animals into humans are called shapeshifters. Princes and princesses often start out as frogs before magically turning into a handsome prince or a beautiful princess, as happens in the European fairy story, "The Frog Princess."

Little Briar Rose

This popular fairy story by the Brothers Grimm is known today as "Sleeping Beauty."

Once upon a time, a king and queen ruled in a land where there were thirteen fairies. The king and queen had no children. Each day, they wished that they might be blessed with one.

One day, the queen saw a poor little fish stranded on the river bank. Gently, she put it back into the river.

Before swimming away the fish lifted its head out of the water and said, "As thanks for helping me, you will soon have a daughter."

Italian poet, courtier, and fairy tale collector, Giambattista Basile called this tale, "Sun, Moon, and Talia". The Brothers Grimm retold the fairy story we know today, calling it "Little Briar Rose."

When the queen gave birth to a baby girl, the king was overjoyed. He decided to hold a great feast and invited everyone, including the fairies. Unfortunately, the king had only twelve gold dishes so one fairy was not invited.

At the feast each fairy gave their best gift to the child but, before the twelfth fairy could do so, the thirteenth fairy arrived. In revenge for not being invited, she cried, "When the king's daughter becomes fifteen she will be pricked by a **spindle** and fall down dead."

The twelfth fairy was able to alter the curse slightly by saying, "She will not die, but she will sleep for a hundred years."

The fearful king had all the spindles in the land burnt! By the time the princess was fifteen, the curse had been forgotten.

On her birthday, the princess explored the castle and discovered an old woman in a turret room spinning yarn on a spindle. She asked if she might try. In an instant, her finger was pricked. Feeling tired, she went to lie down and fell asleep.

Every living thing in the castle also fell asleep and a large hedge of thorns grew around the castle so that people trying to get inside were torn to pieces.

One day, a hundred years later, a prince, hearing about the curse, decided to investigate. By this time, the curse had lifted and he got into the castle easily. When he found the princess, he fell in love with her on sight. It took one kiss to wake her, and do you know what happened? They married and lived happily ever after.

Rhodopis

This is a tale about a red-cheeked Greek slave girl who lived in the land of the pharaohs.

There was once a Greek slave girl named Rhodopis who worked for a kind old master. The other servant girls made her do most of the work and teased her about her pale skin that burnt in the sun.

At the end of each day, Rhodopis walked down to the river where her friends the animals greeted her. The birds fed from her hands and a monkey sat on her shoulder. Often she would dance and sing on the golden sand of the river bank.

One day her master, who had been sleeping under a tree, awoke to see Rhodopis dancing. He was so delighted that he gave her a pair of red slippers.

"Such a talented dancer must wear shoes," he said.

Soon after this, the pharaoh held a feast and all the people in the kingdom were invited. The servant girls put on their finest clothes but gave Rhodopis so many chores to do that she had to stay home. The next day, Rhodopis was washing clothes in the river. She left her slippers on the bank so they would not get wet.

Suddenly the god Horus, disguised as a falcon, swooped down and snatched one of the red slippers. He flew to the feast and dropped it in the pharaoh's lap. The pharaoh believed he should marry whoever the slipper belonged to, and he searched the kingdom from end to end.

Eventually, he came to the house of Rhodopis's master. As he stepped off his barge, the servant girls dashed out in their fine clothes to try on the slipper. But it did not fit. Looking around, the pharaoh saw Rhodopis hiding in the **papyrus** reeds. He beckoned her over. When the slipper fit perfectly, the pharaoh decreed they would marry. The whole kingdom was invited to attend their wedding.

The story of Rhodopis is similar to the later European tale, "Cinderella," whose slippers are made of glass.

Andromeda

This is an ancient story of a prince, a princess, and a monster sea serpent.

A long, long time ago in ancient Ethiopia, there lived a **vain** and silly queen named Cassiopeia and her beautiful daughter Andromeda. One day, Cassiopeia boasted that they were more beautiful than all the Nereids, who were the **nymph-** daughters of the sea god Nereus.

When Poseidon, the ruling god of the sea, heard this he sent the monster sea serpent Cetus to destroy the kingdom as a punishment. After half the kingdom had been destroyed, Cassiopeia and her husband King Cepheus consulted a wise oracle who told them the only way to stop the destruction was to sacrifice Andromeda to the sea monster.

So Andromeda was chained to a rock by the sea and left to await her dreadful fate.

The story of Andromeda has similarities to "St George and the dragon," in which the hero saves a princess from a dragon.

Luckily the Greek hero Perseus happened to be flying nearby. He had just killed the **gorgon** Medusa. As he approached Andromeda, he saw the sea monster about to attack the helpless princess. Wasting no time, he used his winged sandals to dive down swiftly to the monster.

Medusa had a nest of snakes for hair. Anything that looked upon her face was turned to stone, even after her head had been cut off.

As Andromeda turned away, Perseus pulled Medusa's head from a bag and thrust it toward the serpent. Cetus immediately turned to stone and sank beneath the waves.

Perseus freed Andromeda, then married her. They lived happily ever after in Greece and had seven sons and two daughters.

Princess of the Mist

This is a story from North America about the brave Ojibwa princess Green Mantle.

Long ago, in Canada, there lived a peace-loving chief of the Ojibwa. One day, he learned from his scouts that a large war party of Sioux warriors were looking for his tribe.

"Our warriors are too few and I am too old to fight," he said to his only daughter. "Tell me, Green Mantle, what I should do."

Green Mantle thought a while and came up with a plan, but she did not tell her father. That night she crept away and paddled several miles up the Kaministiquia River.

Eventually, she came upon the Sioux camp and was captured.

The Ojibwa are one of the largest groups of Native Americans. They are members of the First Nations peoples.

The princess pretended to be afraid and promised to show the Sioux where her people were if they spared her life. The warriors agreed. The next morning, they set off with Princess Green Mantle in the lead canoe.

The Sioux warriors did not know the area and were easily led by the princess down the river to Kakabeka Falls. By the time the Sioux realized the danger they were in, it was too late. Every canoe plunged into the gorge and the princess died along with all the warriors. Her self-sacrifice had saved her people from certain death.

The princess can sometimes be seen in the mist of Kakabeka Falls.

The Frog Prince

This fairy tale about a frog and a princess is based on the original story collected by the Brothers Grimm.

One hot sunny day, a princess was walking in the forest throwing a golden ball in the air and catching it. As she passed an old well, the ball slipped from her grasp and rolled into the well.

"Oh, my favorite toy!" she wailed. "I shall never see it again."

"Maybe I can help," said a frog sitting on the edge of the well. "What will you give me if I fetch your golden ball?"

"You may have whatever you desire, dear frog. My jewels, even my golden crown."

"I do not want riches," replied the frog. "But if you will love me and let me eat with you and sleep in your bed and be your friend, then I will fetch your toy."

"Oh, yes! I promise all you ask," said the princess.

At that, the frog dived into the well and retrieved the golden ball. When the ball was in her hands, the princess ran off without saying a word to the frog. The frog hopped after her and followed her to a castle.

The princess ran into the dining room and slammed the door behind her. Shortly afterward, there was a knocking at the door.

"Who is that?" asked the king.

The princess told him about the frog.

"A promise is a promise," the king said.

The princess opened the door and lifted the frog onto the table, barely hiding her disgust. After the frog had eaten, he asked to be taken to her bedroom since by now it was bedtime.

The princess made him sleep on a couch but, in the night, the frog crept into her bed for warmth. When the princess awoke in the morning and saw the frog, she screamed and threw him against the wall. In that instant, the frog changed into a handsome prince. "You have released me from the witch's curse!" he cried. And the very next day the whole kingdom rejoiced at their wedding.

The term "Fairy Tales" was first used by Countess d'Aulnoy (1650–1705), a French writer of fairy stories.

The Princess and the Pea

This is a Scandinavian fairy story about a sad prince and a sensitive princess.

Once upon a time, there was a prince who lived in a castle in a faraway land. The prince wanted desperately to marry a princess. He had traveled the whole world looking for one, but there was always something wrong with them. Often they said they were princesses but it was so difficult to know if they were telling the truth.

So at last he returned home, but without a princess to marry, he was very unhappy. Then, shortly after his return, there was a terrible storm. It thundered and there was lightning and it poured down with rain. In the middle of the storm, there was a loud knocking at the town gate and the old king went to answer it himself.

Standing at the gate was a bedraggled young woman, with water running down from her hair and soaked clothes. She had gotten lost in the storm and pleaded for shelter. What a sight she looked, and yet she said she was a princess!

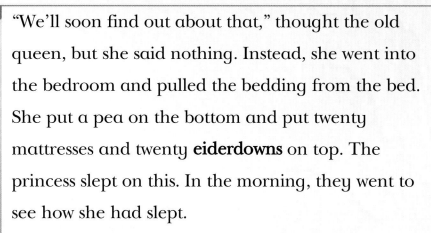

"We'll soon find out about that," thought the old queen, but she said nothing. Instead, she went into the bedroom and pulled the bedding from the bed. She put a pea on the bottom and put twenty mattresses and twenty **eiderdowns** on top. The princess slept on this. In the morning, they went to see how she had slept.

"Oh, terribly," she said. "I have hardly slept a wink all night. I must have been lying on something hard, for I am black and blue all over!"

Now they knew she was truly a princess because she felt the pea through all those mattresses. Nobody but a real princess could be as sensitive as that. So the prince married her and the pea was put in a museum where it can still be seen, if it hasn't been stolen...

"The Princess and the Pea" was first written down by Hans Christian Anderson, a famous Danish author of many fairy tales.

Snow White

This famous fairy story from Germany was collected by the Brothers Grimm.

There was once a wicked, vain queen who had a stepdaughter named Snow White. Every day, the queen asked her magic mirror, "Magic mirror in my hand, who is the fairest in the land?"

The mirror always replied, "My queen, you are the fairest in the land."

But one day the mirror replied, "My queen, you are the fairest here so true. But Snow White is a thousand times more beautiful than you."

From that day on, the queen became green with envy and she felt only hatred for Snow White. Eventually, she ordered a huntsman to take Snow White to the forest and kill her and to return with her heart. The huntsman, being a good fellow, let Snow White go and returned to the queen with a boar's heart.

In the original story the queen demanded the lungs and liver of Snow White!

Snow White wandered the forest until she came upon a cottage where seven dwarves lived. They adopted her as their very own big sister.

Meanwhile, the queen asked her mirror once again and was shocked to hear, "Snow White beyond the mountains at the seven dwarves' is a thousand times more beautiful than you."

The evil queen then tried twice to kill Snow White. Both times the dwarves were able to revive her. On the third attempt, disguised as an old woman, the queen offered Snow White half an apple she had poisoned. While the queen ate the unpoisoned half, Snow White took one bite and collapsed. This time, the dwarves were unable to save her and so they placed her body in a coffin made of glass.

One day, a prince who was traveling the land saw the coffin and fell in love with Snow White. Just then, the servants holding the coffin stumbled, causing the piece of apple to dislodge from Snow White's throat. The prince immediately declared his love for her and all the kings and queens were invited to the wedding. And what about the evil queen? She died a very horrible death.

Originally, the queen was Snow White's mother. The Grimms changed her into an evil stepmother.

Princess Savitri

This is a story of how an Indian princess saved her husband from the god of death.

Legend has it that a long time ago there lived a beautiful princess named Savitri who fell in love with Prince Satyavan. She had been told by a holy **seer** that the prince had only a year to live, but she still insisted on marrying him.

The prince was blissfully unaware of his future and the couple lived happily for a year. On the day of his death, the prince went to the woods with his axe. Princess Savitri insisted on going with him.

Yama is the god of death. He collects the souls of people who have died.

While the princess rested, the prince chopped firewood. Suddenly, he dropped to his knees. Savitri helped him to lie down in the shade of a tree. The prince's eyes closed.

Savitri looked up. A scary man had appeared. His skin was darker than night and his eyes glowed bright red. "Who are you?" she asked.

"I am Yama. I have come to take Prince Satyavan's spirit," he replied, and passing a small thread through the prince's body, he drew out the prince's soul.

Then Yama turned and headed back to his domain. Princess Savitri followed him.

"Princess, you cannot follow me to the land of the dead!" he said, looking back.

"My duty is to stay with my husband."

"Princess, that duty is finished now. Still, your loyalty does you credit. I will grant you a wish, but you cannot ask for the life of your husband."

"Then I wish to have many children. And let them be Satyavan's children!"

Yama realized that he would have to release the soul of the prince to keep the promise he had made.

"Princess, you are as clever as you are brave," Yama said, and he released the soul of the prince.

And that is how the brave and clever Princess Savitri saved her prince from an early death.

Rapunzel

This famous fairy story was discovered in Italy in 1637 by Giambattista Basile.

One day, a long time ago, a pregnant woman sent her husband to fetch some rapunzel from the witch's garden. But the witch caught the husband stealing the plants! In his terror, he promised to give their child to the witch after it was born.

Later that year, his wife gave birth to a beautiful daughter whom they named Rapunzel, after the plant. When Rapunzel was twelve, the witch took the child. She hid her away in a tower that had no door or stairs.

Rapunzel had beautiful long hair that she kept braided. When the witch visited every day, she called up to Rapunzel, "Rapunzel, Rapunzel, let down your fair hair."

Rapunzel let down her braided hair so that the witch could climb up.

Rapunzel is the name for a plant with a parsnip-like root that was used like a radish. In earlier versions, Rapunzel is named Petrosinella after parsley.

One day, a prince rode by and heard Rapunzel singing. He fell in love with her but he could not find a way into the tower. When he saw the witch calling out to her, he discovered the secret.

"Rapunzel, Rapunzel, let down your fair hair," the prince called out.

When Rapunzel saw him she, too, fell in love. A few days later, they decided to escape. The prince returned that night with a horse. Meanwhile, Rapunzel made a rope from sheets.

But Rapunzel told the witch how much easier it was to pull up the prince. The witch, in a fury, cut off Rapunzel's hair and abandoned her in a wild and terrible place.

When the prince arrived, the witch attached Rapunzel's hair to a hook and let it down. Taken by surprise, the prince was hurled from the tower. When he landed in the thorns below, he was blinded.

For several months, he wandered the land until one day he heard a familiar voice singing. It was Rapunzel! When they embraced, her tears of joy fell into his eyes and cured his blindness. They returned to his home and married and lived happily ever after.

GLOSSARY

eiderdowns Quilts or coverings stuffed for warmth with the down, or soft feathers, of an eider duck

gorgon A terrifying female creature from ancient Greece. There were three gorgons and they were sisters.

nymph A spirit of nature in ancient Greek mythology, who is usually beautiful and young

papyrus An Egyptian water plant from which paper was made

seer A person who has the gift of seeing into the future

spindle A tapered pin at one end with a weight at the other, on which fibers are spun by hand into thread

vain Too proud of one's good looks

INDEX